This Is the CONSTRUCTION WORKER

By Laura Godwin   Pictures by Julian Hector

𝔇𝔦𝔰𝔫𝔢𝔶 • HYPERION

LOS ANGELES   NEW YORK

For Imari Jane Cross
—L.G.

For my best friend, Lindsey
—J.H.

First Edition, May 2019

10 9 8 7 6 5 4 3 2 1

FAC-029191-19039

Printed in Malaysia

This book is set in Goudy Old Style/Monotype

Designed by Maria Elias

Library of Congress Cataloging-in-Publication Data

Names: Godwin, Laura, author. • Hector, Julian, illustrator.

Title: This is the construction worker / by Laura Godwin ; pictures by Julian Hector.

Description: First edition. • Los Angeles ; New York : Disney Hyperion, 2019.

Summary: Illustrations and easy-to-read, rhyming text follow a

construction worker and her crew through a day of drilling, digging,

crawling, and clanging.

Identifiers: LCCN 2018032567 • ISBN 9781368018173 (hardcover)

• ISBN 1368018173 (hardcover)

Subjects: • CYAC: Stories in rhyme. • Construction workers—Fiction.

Building—Fiction.

Classification: LCC PZ8.3.G5465 Tf 2019 • DDC [E]—dc23

LC record available at https://lccn.loc.gov/2018032567

Reinforced binding

Visit www.DisneyBooks.com

This is the construction worker.
These are her clothes.

This is the hard hat.
And boots—
with steel toes!

These are the gloves
and the bright orange vest.
This is the tool belt—
and now she is dressed!

This is the truck
that drives to the site.
These are machines that
sat quiet all night.

This is the foreman,
the boss of the crew,
who tells all the workers
what they need to do.

This is the dump truck.
This is the load.
This is the gravel
it dumps on the road.

This is the beam.
This is the space.
This is the crane
that will hoist it in place.

This is the scaffold
that reaches the sky.
This is the *clang*
and the *bang*
and the cry—

And now comes the moment
they all love the best,
when each of the workers
sits down for a rest.

Then each of those workers at work once again—

walking and riding,

pushing and sliding,

drilling and screwing

and painting and gluing.

Hauling and rigging

and crawling and digging,

pounding and banging

and bashing and clanging.

This is the grind of the gears
and the smell of the diesel and oil.

These are the shouts and the cheers.
This is the sound of the toil.

This is the glint
of the steel.
This is the hint of the spire.
This is the sun on the beams
and the girders that climb
ever higher.

From sunup to sundown
they know what to do,
each of the workers—
a part of the crew!